WHICH WAY, DUDE?

#1

BMO's D___ ___

WHICH WAY, DUDE?

#1

BMO's Day Out

by Max Brallier
illustrated by Stephen Reed

PSS!
PRICE STERN SLOAN
An Imprint of Penguin Group (USA) Inc.

Grosset & Dunlap
Published by the Penguin Group
Penguin Group (USA) Inc., 375 Hudson Street, New York, New York 10014, USA

USA | Canada | UK | Ireland | Australia | New Zealand | India | South Africa | China
Penguin Books Ltd, Registered Offices: 80 Strand, London WC2R 0RL, England

For more information about the Penguin Group visit penguin.com

Published in 2013 by Price Stern Sloan, a division of Penguin Young Readers Group,
345 Hudson Street, New York, New York 10014. PSS! is a registered trademark of
Penguin Group (USA) Inc. Printed in the U.S.A.

ISBN 978-0-8431-7327-7   10 9 8 7 6 5 4 3 2 1

THE FUTURE OF THE LAND OF OOO IS IN YOUR HANDS!

Hey there!

It's me, BMO—the cutest, tiniest little robot in the Land of Ooo. Me and a few of my radical buddies are going on an adventure, and *you're* going to decide what happens!

This book is *not* like most books... At the end of every chapter, you'll have a choice to make—and sometimes you'll have to solve puzzles to help figure out what I should do!

Along the way you'll earn **ADVENTURE MINUTES**. Adventure Minutes are like proof of how awesome your journey was. The more Adventure Minutes you earn, the greater and more kick-butt your journey! Whenever you earn Adventure Minutes, flip to page 121 so you can keep track of them. When you come to an ending, add up all your Adventure Minutes to determine your total **ADVENTURE TIME!**

Good luck!

And remember... the future of the Land of Ooo is in *your* hands!

BEGINNINGS
AND STUFF!

"This is BUNK!" Finn is squeezing his game controller with furious Finn frustration. Beside him, Jake grins as he taps his controller. The two best buds are playing *Portender Defender* on their video-game system, BMO.

But BMO is more than just Finn and Jake's video-game system. BMO is also a camera, a flashlight, and—*most important of all*—a radical friend! BMO is tiny and blue and ridiculously cute. So cute that if you want to say "Hey, that's cute," you might as well just say "Hey, that's BMO." In fact, yes, you should start doing that.

Jake flexes his rubbery muscles in triumph. "You shouldn't have challenged me in *Portender Defender*, bro. I am the *king* of *Portender Defender*. I even have a crown. See?" Just like that, Jake's rubbery head changes into a yellow crown.

Finn frowns. "That's not a real crown. That's a fleshy head crown. Fleshy head crowns don't count."

"Better a fleshy head crown than no crown," Jake says, leaning back happily. "And you have *no* crowns."

Finn is trying to come back with a killer burn when he's interrupted by—

TAP! TAP! TAP!

Someone at the front door . . .

Finn leaps to his feet. A knock at the front door usually means *adventure*. Or sometimes Gumdrop Scout cookies. But most of the time, yeah, adventure. Really, either would be fine, because gumdrop cookies are lumping delectable. Finn sprints to the door and yanks it open, revealing the short, round, red-and-white Candy Kingdom servant known as Peppermint Butler (or Pep-But, for short).

"Pep-But!" Finn exclaims. "What are you doing so far from the Candy Kingdom?"

Peppermint Butler is out of breath. "It's Princess Bubblegum—" he says, struggling to catch his breath. "Princess Bubblegum is in—"

"In what?" Finn asks. "In bed? In the hospital? In a new movie!?"

Jake whispers to Finn, "Dude, your guesses are terrible. Also, Peppermint Butler is pretty out of shape. We should get him on a cardio routine."

Peppermint Butler finally spits out, "Princess Bubblegum is **in trouble**!"

Finn's eyes go as wide as flying saucers. "PB? PB needs me?"

"Hey, that rhymed," Jake says. "Twice."

"Fill me in on the situation and junk, Pep-But," Finn says.

"She appears to be in a trance," Pep-But says as he steps inside. "She is not herself. She has locked many Candy People away in the dungeons. Other citizens have fled."

Jake frowns. "Whoa, PB is tyrannical."

"Someone or *something* must be controlling her," Finn

4

says. "Some *foul creature!*"

Not far away, watching this conversation go down, is BMO. And right now, BMO is *amped up*, because it's clear an adventure is about to happen. Radical adventures are always getting started in the Tree Fort. Just looking around, BMO can see all sorts of evidence of Finn and Jake's kick-butt hero adventures throughout the Land of Ooo: monster-skin rugs and piles of gold and old swords and pearly white skulls.

But BMO never gets to be the hero, and that's bunk! "Today will be different!" BMO declares.

Yes, today, BMO will do some butt punching! *This day* will be BMO's adventure day . . .

Pep-But heads back to the kingdom to deal with the crisis while Finn gets dressed for action. He throws on his backpack and grabs his Demon sword. "You know what time it is?" Finn asks Jake.

"Pretty sure it's time for a nap." Jake yawns. "I'm all tuckered out from crushing you in *Portender Defender.*"

Finn stares at Jake very seriously. "No, dude."

Jake sighs. "Oh, right. Yeah, yeah, adventure time . . ."

A frown is displayed on BMO's screen as the tiny robot waddles over to Finn and Jake and asks, very softly, "Can I also have an adventure time?"

Finn and Jake exchange nervous glances. Finn kneels down and says, "BMO, you know I love you. But you're *tiny.* And the danger we face is **BIG**. This adventure probably isn't for you."

Jake pats BMO on the head. "Don't worry, homie, we'll be back in no time!"

Finn waves good-bye, and the door slams shut. BMO climbs

up on a chair and peers out the window. It's a gigantic lumping world *full of adventure*, just ready for the taking.

And BMO is stuck inside, all alone!

Total stupid garbage!

"Not today!" BMO exclaims. "I will have an adventure. Today, BMO will be *BMO THE BRAVE!*"

But where will this adventure begin?

If you think BMO should try to catch up to Finn and Jake and join in on the fun, **TURN TO PAGE 21**

If you think BMO should set off on a solo adventure, **TURN TO PAGE 82**

If you think BMO is sad and confused and needs a little alone time to figure out this desperate need to be a hero, **TURN TO PAGE 76**

BAD
HAIR DAY

BMO exits the maze of hair and comes out—*oh no*—in Princess Bubblegum's sandbox! BMO ran the wrong way.

And Princess Bubblegum's sandbox isn't just a normal place for doing fun sandy stuff . . . Princess Bubblegum does *experiments* in her sandbox—whacked-out mad scientist experiments . . .

There is a sudden flash of light—a lamp is shining down on BMO. BMO looks up. It's PB! And she's holding a bunch of strange metal tools. "Hello, BMO," Princess Bubblegum says, as she snaps open a pair of supersharp silver scissors. "Are you ready to play science?"

And then, Princess Bubblegum leans over and begins cutting . . .

THE END

WRONG
ME-MOW!

BMO swings at the Me-Mow on the far left.

Uh-oh . . .

BMO *misses!*

That was *not* the real Me-Mow!

Me-Mow howls with evil laughter—*so evil!*—and then leaps up, bounces off BMO's head, and soars towards Jake! *INCOMING ASSASSIN!*

Me-Mow lands on Jake's head. Her creepy kitten eyes narrow, she raises her paw, and she *jams* the tiny poisoned needle into Jake's arm.

"Ow!" Jake cries out. "That *hurt!*"

"You are now poisoned!" Me-Mow hisses. "I'm going to take you back to the Guild of Assassins and prove my worth!"

Jake eyes are looking *sleepy.* "Man, it's tired out here," Jake mutters. "I could use a little nap. But first, I need to—"

CLONK!

Jake collapses on the ground! The poison has put him to sleep! And if BMO and Finn can't save him soon, he'll be asleep—*FOREVER!*

Me-Mow throws Jake's leg over her shoulder and runs into the brush, dragging Jake behind her.

Finn is waking up and rubbing his noggin when he realizes Jake is gone. "*What the what?* Me-Mow stole Jake!"

BMO sulks. "I am sorry, Finn. I nose-dived."

Finn pats the tiny robot on the head. "You didn't, um, *nose-dive*, BMO. We just gotta hurry to rescue Jake!"

BMO and Finn bolt through the forest and into the brush. They both look around, frantic, but Me-Mow is gone, and Jake is nowhere to be seen!

"Stupid kitten . . ." Finn moans.

But BMO's radical robot eyes spot something. "Finn, do not worry. I see a trail of tiny Me-Mow paw prints."

Finn squints. BMO is right! He sees a path of tiny kitten prints in the mud, stretching out into the woods. But there are *tons* of footprints. "Oh no," Finn says, "that cat is *good*. There are footprints everywhere! I can barely tell which ones are which!"

HELP BMO AND FINN TRACK DOWN ME-MOW AND JAKE

Me-Mow's footprints are everywhere!
On the next page, pick out the footprints that
all travel in one direction and follow them to the
next part of BMO's adventure!

9

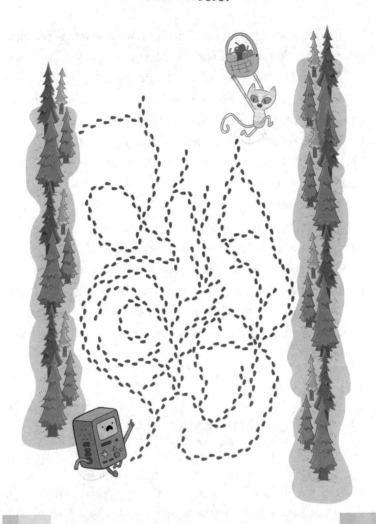

If you ended up at the forest, **TURN TO PAGE 15**

If you ended up at Me-Mow, **TURN TO PAGE 37**

NEXT SOUL, PLEASE!

BMO does something very much unlike BMO! BMO turns away from the helpless Finn and says to Death, "I will take one soul, please."

Death smiles. "Okay, then I shall *spin the wheel of souls*!"

Death snaps his fingers and a giant wheel appears out of thin air. "Here we go!"

He gives it a hard spin and the wheel is suddenly a blur of souls! After what feels like an eternity, it began to slow down. *Tick, tick, tick, tick, tick* . . .

At last, it stops. BMO's eyes are wide. The soul is ready. And it is . . .

BILLY!

BMO is staring at an image of Billy, the greatest warrior of all time. Billy is radical—the awesome Billy song says it all. It goes a little something like:

Who's the greatest warrior ever?

A hero of renown?

Who slayed an Evil Ocean?

Who cast the Lich down?

BILLY!

And that time the evil Fire Count

Captured a damsel fair,

Who saved her with such brav'ry

She offered him her hair?

BILLY!

Also . . . he fought a bear!

BILLY!

So, yeah—Billy is awesome. BMO stares at the soul with wide eyes. "I get Billy's soul? The soul of the greatest warrior ever?"

Death nods slowly. "Yes, that is the soul the wheel has chosen for you."

Death waves his hand around and does some cool magic death junk, and then—*FLASH!*—Billy's soul is *yanked* from the wheel and transported into BMO's tiny robot body.

Suddenly, BMO feels very different. BMO feels *strong.*

BMO = Billy.

Billy = BMO.

The greatest warrior of all time is now a tiny robot.

And Finn? Sadly, Finn is about to be crushed by the strange Worm Creature!

FRIED
BMO!

ZAP!!!

Electricity shoots through BMO's body, and the tiny robot shakes and sizzles! BMO's screen goes totally blank as BMO's legs give out and the tiny robot collapses.

"BMO!" Marceline exclaims.

BMO's screen flashes twice, then displays a hundred little dots.

"BMO! Are you okay?" Melissa asks. "What's happening?"

But BMO says nothing. BMO does not even move . . .

"I think BMO is, like, rebooting or some junk," Marceline says.

HELP BRING BMO BACK ONLINE!

On the next page, can you cross all nine circuits using only four lines, without lifting your pencil? If you lift your pencil, the connection will be broken and BMO will be lost forever!

Be careful, you only get one try . . .

If you can do it, TURN TO PAGE 107

If you don't think it can be done, TURN TO PAGE 70

TIME IS UP
FOR JAKE!

Finn and BMO come out at the forest at the end of the maze of footprints and—*oh no!*—they're staring at a giant stone wall!

Finn throws up his hands. "We're at a dead end! Jake will be lost for good!"

Alas, it is true. Jake is now in the hands of Me-Mow, evil kitten assassin. And the poison is quickly sucking the life out of the magic dog . . .

BMO sheds a single, solitary, digital tear.

BMO has failed.

And now . . .

Jake

Is

Dead!!!

THE END

STRANGE STUFF
BEHIND CASTLE WALLS...

BMO, Finn, and Jake wander through the Cotton Candy Forest, where the trees are made of sugary deliciousness. It's a superslow walk, mainly because Jake can't go five feet without stretching his arms out and grabbing a chunk to chow down on.

It's nearly sunset when the gang first spies the Candy Kingdom. BMO sees the sugary pink mountains that surround the kingdom; then, as they exit the forest, BMO sees Princess Bubblegum's castle, made all of vanilla! High in the sky is the great puff of sugary frosting that tops the castle's enormous central tower. Great spires of upside-down ice-cream cones point toward the sky.

It's an awesome, amazing, and totally *tasty* sight.

But something doesn't feel right . . . BMO can tell something *very not good* is going on.

There is a *ton* of Candy People outside the city walls! Weirdest of all, the Gumball Guardians—gigantic candy creatures who are usually perched on the castle walls—are sitting in the yellow grass outside the castle. They seem to be guarding the drawbridge (made of toast covered with berry jam) that crosses the cherry-soda moat.

"Weirdness," Finn says.

"Yeah, what's going down?" Jake wonders.

As the gang approaches, the first Gumball Guardian verrrry slowwwwly rises to his feet. "Halt!" the Gumball Guardian bellows in a deep, robotic voice.

Jake is offended! "Hey, it's *us*. You know, the guys. We're pretty much honorary Candy Kingdom citizens."

"Yeah, we're pals with Princess Bubblegum," Finn says.

"By order of Princess Bubblegum," the Gumball Guardian says, *"no one shall enter the castle."*

Luckily, Peppermint Butler spies what's going down and runs toward the gang before a ginormous rumble breaks out. "Oh, thank the candy heavens, you made it!"

BMO steps forward proudly. "Of course I made it. When BMO the Brave is called upon, BMO the Brave shows up—rain, sleet, or snowball fight."

Finn and Jake giggle.

BMO continues, "Now, if I'm going to save the Kingdom, I need to know exactly what's going on behind those giant candy walls. Jake, lift me!"

Jake grabs hold of BMO, his legs get all super-*extendy*, and he lifts BMO high up into the air. BMO grabs hold of the castle wall and peeks over the side. And what BMO sees is *terrifying* . . .

There are worms *everywhere*. An entire army of them: worms chilling at the Candy Tavern, worms sweeping the streets, worms digging graves, worms just hanging out being worms! And these worms are *bad!*

Jake lowers BMO back down. Finn and Jake listen with horror as BMO reports on the terrible sights inside the castle

17

walls. "The King Worm must be behind this!" Finn exclaims.

"This is no time for talk," BMO declares. "We must unlock the gate from the inside and take back the castle! Jake, turn the crank and raise the gate. And you do not blow this one!"

HELP JAKE UNLOCK THE CASTLE GATE

Navigate Jake's rubbery arm past the Worm Guards without getting caught. But remember, once you choose a path, there's no turning back!

BMO's Day Out

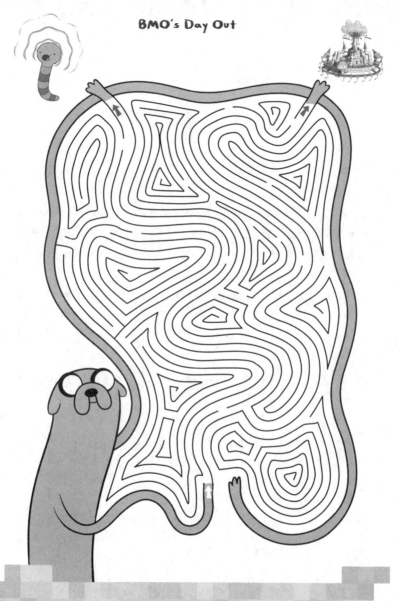

If you ended up at the castle, **TURN TO PAGE 28**

If you ended up at the worm, **TURN TO PAGE 39**

ESCAPE!

BMO tiptoes down the hall. The Banana Guards were so blinded by the superbright flash, they didn't even notice BMO nab the key and sneak out! BMO heads straight for Princess Bubblegum's bedroom.

But even from the hall, BMO can see a tall shadow looming over the Princess's bed . . .

The King Worm . . .

★ ★ **BMO earns 48 ADVENTURE MINUTES.** ★ ★

To continue the adventure, **TURN TO PAGE 46**

CATCHING UP
WITH FINN AND JAKE

"I will follow Finn and Jake," BMO decides. "I will help them be heroes, and I will be a star!"

BMO runs outside and shuts the door tight, because BMO is responsible like that.

Scanning the horizon, BMO sees no sign of Finn and Jake . . .

Which way would they have gone?

Duh! The Candy Kingdom! Way, way far-off in the distance, BMO can see the tip-top of the giant tree that forms the center of Princess Bubblegum's Candy Castle.

"I'm a serious hero," BMO declares and takes off running. "I'm all, like, 'show me the trouble and I will fix it, tough guy.' That's the kind of hero I am."

Just outside the Verdant Plains, near the border of the Burning Lands, BMO slides to a stop. The tiny robot hears something.

KLANG! KRASH!

Fighting sounds from just over the hill! Fighting sounds are like the *call of adventure*! BMO hears the *SMACK* of a butt being punched and then a deafening *KRAK* that definitely maybe sounds like Finn crashing through a tree.

BMO scrambles up the hill as fast as a tiny robot can scramble, then crawls to the edge of a small rock ledge, peers

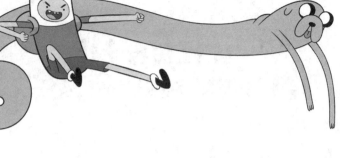

through the trees, and sees action. *Serious action.*

It's Me-Mow, the tiny cat assassin! Finn and Jake have their hands full . . . Me-Mow is serious bad stuff: One time, Me-Mow almost *killed* Jake while trying to assassinate Wildberry Princess. Has the killer kitten returned to finish the job?

BMO watches the action . . .

"I think it's time for a Jake shot!" Finn cries out, and Jake *transforms* into a **slingshot.** Jake's elastic yellow body stretches all rubber-like, and his gut pulls back, *back, BACK,* forming a small seat. Finn climbs up onto Jake and sits in the chubby gut seat.

"Ready, dude?" Jake asks.

"Ready, dude," Finn says.

Together the buds cry out *"JAKE SHOT!"* and Jake's rubbery yellow body flings Finn forward through the air, *just like a slingshot.* Finn is on a direct collision course with Me-Mow!

"Say your prayers, kitten!" Finn yells.

But no! A split-second before Finn collides with Me-Mow, the cat springs into the air. Finn soars underneath the leaping cat and, instead of colliding with Me-Mow, slams headfirst into a rock. Finn gets to his feet, stumbles around for a moment, and then tumbles over.

Me-Mow isn't finished! The killer kitten soars through the air and clonks Jake on the head!

"That cat is a butt!" BMO declares. It's time for—*dun, dun, DUN!*—BMO the Brave!

BMO waddles to the ledge and shouts, as loudly as the tiny robot can shout, "Hey, little cat assassin. Why don't you punch someone your own size?"

★ ★ **BMO** earns 4 ADVENTURE MINUTES. ★ ★

Uh-oh! It's about to get fighty up in here!
TURN TO PAGE 44

HELP
ARRIVES

"Hey, Death, what gives!? Give us back our little buddy!" Finn shouts.

This does not make Death happy . . . Death throws down his controller and shouts "Not until I beat this game!"

"I really think you should take a break," BMO whispers to Death. "You've been playing a while. For, like, maybe years . . ."

"You don't tell me when I've played long enough! I tell you!" And with that, Death *roars!* Suddenly, skeleton dudes are *everywhere*—coming over the hills and crawling out of the ground.

"Get them!" Death shouts to his skeleton army.

Finn *flies* through the air with his sword raised and chops the two closest skeleton dudes in half while Jake lands a pair of rubbery punches.

BMO leaps up and runs toward Finn and Jake. "Finn! I am coming!"

Together, the trio darts through the gathering crowd of ferocious skeleton people.

"There's the portal to back home!" Jake points. "Just over the hill!"

But there are skeleton people *everywhere.*

Finn's eyes dart back and forth. Finally, Finn says, "BMO, you know this place better than we do now. You lead the way!"

HELP BMO LEAD HIS FRIENDS OUT OF THE LAND OF THE DEAD!

On the next page, navigate the maze to find the path to freedom! But be careful—once you choose a path, there's no turning back!

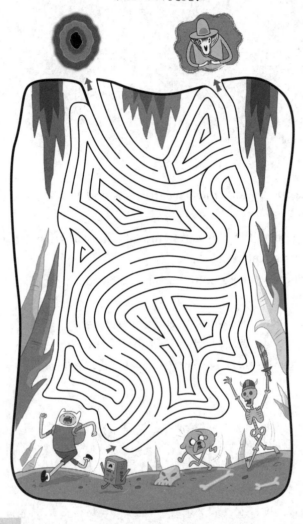

If you ended up at the portal, **TURN TO PAGE 53**

If you ended up at Death, **TURN TO PAGE 67**

POWER SLAPS
DO ROCK!

Jake gives one final, furious thunderclap, and the rock monster explodes!

BMO grins. "My plan was awesome."

The trio sprints past the defeated rock monster. A final skeleton *lunges* as they come to the end of the path, and it grabs BMO with its cold, skeletal fingers.

"Oh no you *don't*," Finn shouts as he **kicks** the skeleton in the head, popping its skull off its neck bone.

BMO takes a last look at the Land of the Dead and sees Death hot on their tail! And then, they leap through the portal—

TURN TO PAGE 118 to get back to the Land of Ooo!

GATE = UNLOCKED!

"Got it!" Jake exclaims. His hand grips the crank and turns it superslowly—because if they alert the worms, they'll be up to their necks in worm trouble. The gate raises and the drawbridge lowers.

"Now what?" Finn whispers to BMO.

BMO's eyes narrow, and the tiny robot goes into ultraserious action-leader-general mode. "Now? Now, we take back the Candy Kingdom."

And that's a radical plan. Totally. But, before BMO's plan can even get kicking, a figure appears on the castle bridge. A figure in a long dress with a hair like a giant pink blanket. It is— Princess Bubblegum.

"PB!" Finn exclaims. "**There** you are! *What* is going on?"

"You should not be here," Princess Bubblegum says. Her voice is flat as month-old soda.

"Huh?" Finn says.

"Go now, before I must hurt you," she says coolly.

Finn is stunned. He can't believe the whacked-out words coming from his gal pal's mouth! He runs to the bridge, grabs PB by the shoulders, and shakes him. "PB!" Finn cries. "PB, what's wrong with you? *Snap out of it!*"

"Remove your hands from me, Finn Human."

Finn stumbles back. He's so confused. Princess Bubblegum has gone totally nutso crazy. *"WHAT IS HAPPENING TO MY FRIENDS?!!?"* Finn cries out.

BMO watches her carefully before declaring, "She's sleepwalking."

"Sleepwalking?" Finn asks. "Hmm . . . Wait . . . There are worms everywhere, and that one time the King Worm *did* put us all to sleep. I wonder if the King Worm is back and—"

But before Finn can finish his thought, PB steps forward and says, "I've been experimenting. Please meet my newest creation."

Uh-oh . . .

A huge shadow falls over Princess Bubblegum. Something *gigantic* is crawling across the bridge behind her. The shadow becomes larger as this *thing*, whatever it is, exits the castle and goes out into the light. It's something big, something nasty. It is:

The Wormenstein!

It's a fully *gargantuan* worm, almost as tall as the castle walls! And dig this: The Wormenstein is made up *entirely* of other, regular worms! There are thousands upon thousands of tiny little green worms writhing around, somehow joined together by Princess Bubblegum's mad, dark science.

High-pitched shrieks echo across the field as the Candy People lose their cool, big-time. Even Finn, the toughest of the tough, takes a step back. But one citizen of the Land of Ooo shows no fear. One citizen of the Land of Ooo has decided this is not a day for fear but a day for heroics. And that citizen is BMO the Brave.

BMO steps forward and says, as loudly as the tiny robot's little electronic voice box will allow, "Hey, worm jerk, prepare to be hurting."

Jake coughs into his hand and whispers to Finn, "Yo, BMO is super gung-ho today, huh?"

BMO whirls around. "Okay, Finn and Jake, do you know what we need to do now?"

Finn and Jake exchange confused glances, shrug, then look back to BMO.

"Do not worry," BMO says, "I will disclose my daring plan . . ."

FIGURE OUT BMO'S STRATEGY FOR DEFEATING THE WORMENSTEIN!

Find the names of each of these *Adventure Time* characters in the word search. Words go up, down, diagonally, and backward. Unscramble the letters that overlap to find out BMO's plan.

FINN

JAKE

ICE KING

PRINCESS BUBBLEGUM

MARCELINE

DEATH

BMO

LUMPY SPACE PRINCESS

KING WORM

ME-MOW

EARL OF LEMONGRAB

THE LICH

```
L E L V R C A E I G P W Q P A A
U E A R L O F L E M O N G R A B
M R D I R M W S X H N I A I P Y
P X A V Z B Q J I S O A X N M W
Y I J K B G E L F K R S E C A N
S E X H C I C E K I N G L E R P
P T K A E U O F T U N J R S E B
A P H A B R I L O M T Y O S F A
C D K E J E K K J I Q H V B U C
E X I N L K N M H C A T P U W M
P S B T U I I I R P V A S B E K
R A F E E L C N L R P E D B T V
I F D X Z C M H Y E B D E L B H
N Y I B E T E R X V C A C E G Z
C I M N S K M T G L X R N G O V
E E R J N P O B S J E C A U M T
S T U M R O W G N I K M C M N B
S R O Y A B D O I N H T G O A W
```

If you think Jake should transform into a worm,
TURN TO PAGE 90

If you think Jake should transform into a hot dog,
TURN TO PAGE 42

31

iNTO
LuMPY SPACE!

"That . . . is . . . correct . . ." the frog says—and then, suddenly, the frog's eyes open crazy wide and his tongue lashes out and grabs hold of BMO and Marceline and *pulls* them forward. The mouth opens *WIDER* and BMO and Marceline ARE dragged *inside it*.

It's sort of gross . . .

That frog is definitely full of some magic junk or something, because BMO and Marceline now find themselves surrounded by black space and crazy colors: bright yellows and reds and pinks and blues and a whole butt-ton of purple.

They tumble through this strange portal land and into Lumpy Space, where it's all pink and blue clouds, and lumpy stars with long pink tails rocket through the purple sky!

A moment later, they crash onto a lumpy cloud and a Lumpy Space Car slides to a stop beside them. It's a superlumpy convertible—bright pink with purple seats and tiny little lumpy blue wheels. Behind the wheel is LSP's sometimes best friend, Melissa. "Marceline! You made it!"

Marceline does the introductions. "BMO, Melissa. Melissa, BMO. BMO is friends with Finn and Jake."

Melissa is a floating pink blob with bright white eyes and long eyelashes. As she floats out of the car, she blushes and her face goes from pink to, like, superpink. "Oh my glob, you know Finn?" Melissa squeaks. "I LOVE Finn."

BMO steps forward. "Yes, I do know Finn. But I have no time for talk of Finn! I am BMO the Brave, and I am here for adventure! I hear you have an adventure that needs adventuring. Is this true?"

Melissa giggles. "Yup! LSP is going to marry that lumping smooth poser nitwit, the Earl of Lemongrab, and we need to stop it because he's a huge old jerk!"

BMO nods. "Come, let us finish this adventure."

With that, BMO waddles over to the car. Unfortunately, the tiny robot trips on a lumpy puff of cloud and tumbles head over heels.

Melissa frowns. BMO is not exactly inspiring confidence. Melissa pulls Marceline aside. "What happened to Finn and Jake?" Melissa whispers. "You said you were getting Finn and Jake! What gives? This little robot can't help."

"Don't worry, BMO is really good at stuff like this. Just look."

BMO is behind the wheel, standing up very straight on the seat (since it's the only way little BMO can see over the wheel).

Melissa is not sure if this is the greatest idea . . .

★ ★ BMO earns 19 ADVENTURE MINUTES. ★ ★

SOLVE THE PUZZLE TO DECIDE WHO WILL DRIVE!

Who do you think should drive? **BMO** or **Marceline**? Use the key below to substitute each of the characters for one of the letters in each column. It may take a few tries to get it right.

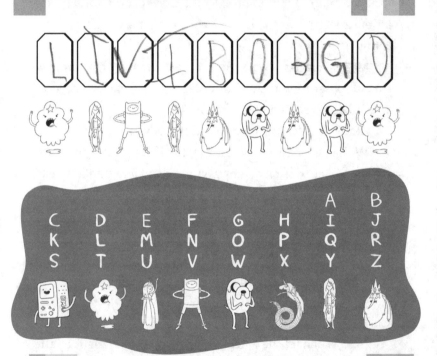

If you agree with Melissa, **TURN TO PAGE 99**

If you disagree with Melissa, **TURN TO PAGE 65**

34

WORMENSTEIN INTO THE MOAT, BMO INTO THE CASTLE

"Into the moat!" BMO orders. "Push the Wormenstein into the moat!"

"Okay!" Jake Worm says, then **pushes**, sending the Wormenstein back, back, *back* toward the moat!

"It's going over!" Finn shouts.

The Candy People cheer as the massive Wormenstein tumbles into the strawberry-soda moat and *bursts* apart. Instead of one giant monster, it is now thousands of individual little green worms—*very annoyed green worms*—floating in the liquid.

Princess Bubblegum is silent for a moment as she watches with creepy vacant eyes. Finally, she turns to her Banana Guards and says softly: *"Get them."*

BMO says to Finn and Jake, "I will sneak inside the castle so I can wake the Princess from her sleepwalking. You hold off the Banana Guards."

"We sure are letting BMO boss us around today, aren't we?" Jake says to Finn.

BMO slips through the charging Banana Guards and beelines it for the castle gate. For once, being tiny is superhelpful—no one notices BMO following the Princess into the castle. Bubblegum glides through the great hall and past the tearoom and finally down a bright orange hallway and into her bedroom. BMO follows . . .

★ ✶ **BMO** *earns* 22 ADVENTURE MINUTES. ★ ✶

Craziness awaits! TURN TO PAGE 46

WATERLOGGED CAT

Nice! BMO and Finn followed the right path! They burst through the bushes and out onto a rocky trail, which runs alongside a steep cliff. A bright blue river rushes by far below. If they stray from the path, they'll be *all wet*.

Finn points and yells, "There!" Me-Mow is dragging Jake through the brush. Jake is snoring like a freight train.

Me-Mow turns and shoots BMO and Finn a dagger-type glare. BMO glares right back and growls, "There is the killer kitten that is now my archenemy. That cat must be declawed."

Me-Mow opens her mouth wide and spits something into her hand. Finn nearly shrieks. It's the antidote to save Jake!

Me-Mow holds it up high. "You dorks come any closer, and I'll throw the antidote into the river!"

Finn and BMO are in a tight spot . . . One false move, and the antidote will be lost forever! And Jake will be lost forever too!

BMO is thinking hard, like a rock. This is the tiny robot's chance to be a true hero. At last, BMO looks up at Finn and says, "Finn, slingshot me, please. Like Jake slingshotted you."

Finn is confused. "Huh? I'm not rubber like Jake. I can't."

"Finn, you do the slingshot to me now!" BMO yells.

"Okay, BMO, if you say so . . ."

Finn picks up BMO, cocks back his arm, and *chucks* the tiny robot! BMO spins and spirals through the air!

"Wha—" Me-Mow exclaims. Before Me-Mow can finish exclaiming stuff—*KA-POW!!!*—BMO slams into the cat assassin and knocks her off her paws. BMO has the cat pinned!

"I'm sitting on you!" BMO says proudly, then hops up and triumphantly yanks the antidote from Me-Mow's hand.

"Hey, Me-Mow, *go fish!*" Finn shouts as he *punts* the killer kitten over the cliff and into the water. It's totally brutal punishment 'cause everyone knows cats hate getting wet.

BMO crouches over the still-snoring Jake and squeezes the liquid antidote into his mouth.

One drop.

Two drops.

Three drops.

Finn holds his breath.

Jake isn't moving! Is it too late?

BMO is about to curse the world, when—

"*Hel-looooo, dudes!*" Jake cries out as he sits upright.

Finn leaps into the air. "He's alive!"

"What happened?" Jake asks. "My head feels all marshmallowy."

Finn smiles. "BMO is a hero, today. *That's* what happened."

"What about Princess Bubblegum?" Jake asks.

"Oh, this adventure is just getting rolling, like a wheel!" BMO says.

★ ✶ **BMO earns 17 ADVENTURE MINUTES.** ★ ✶

Let's keep this adventure going! **TURN TO PAGE 16**

38

JAKE
BLOWS IT!

"Uh-oh," Jake says.

"What did you do, Jake?" Finn asks. Finn has a feeling his buddy just messed up monstrously.

"No one panic, but I think I'm squeezing a worm," Jake says.

Suddenly, a high-pitched alarm goes off! Jake was correct! He was *definitely* squeezing a worm, and that worm *definitely* just alerted Manfried the Talking Piñata aka the Candy Kingdom's alarm system!

"Alert! Alert! Intruders at the entrance to the castle!" Manfried the Talking Piñata announces.

BMO's hands are balled into tiny fists. Trouble is coming, and BMO the Brave is ready.

Suddenly, there is a loud sound from inside the kingdom's walls. It's sort of a wet, sloppy sound.

"Do you hear that?" Finn asks.

"It sounds like a giant worm," Jake says . . .

Just then, the castle gate lifts and the bridge drops. Jake's ears were accurate . . .

TURN TO PAGE 40 to reveal this nasty new danger!

MEET THE KING WORM

It is a *giant* worm—the *giantest* of worms! It is: the KING WORM! The huge worm inches through the gate and out onto the castle bridge. A hundred smaller worms follow behind him.

"Hey guys!" King Worm says, with a creepy mix of enthusiasm and evil.

"King Worm, I should have known," Finn says, grimacing. "You think you can put my friend Princess Bubblegum in a trance and take over the Candy Kingdom? Guess what, jerk, you can't. Let's get him, Jake!"

Jake and Finn charge! But it's no use . . .

WA! WA! WA! WA! WA!

Green energy—*a hundred rays, like lasers!*—blasts out of the King Worm's eyeballs and shoots into Finn's eyes and Jake's eyes and Pep-But's eyes and *everyone's* eyes. Everyone is possessed, just like PB!

Everyone, that is, except BMO . . .

BMO is safe. And not just because is BMO is awesome, but because BMO is a robot and obviously robots

can't be hypnotized by worm energy beams.

"This is perfect," BMO thinks.

BMO will play along . . .

BMO will pretend to be hypnotized so BMO can save the day . . .

★ ✱ **BMO earns** 30 ADVENTURE MINUTES. ★ ✱

To see how BMO will save the day,
TURN TO PAGE 112

41

JAKE
HOT DOG!

"You will become Jake Hot Dog!" BMO announces.

Jake is confused. "Wait, what? You want me to turn into a hot dog? That's the silliest thing I've ever heard—"

"Turn into Jake Hot Dog!" BMO declares. "I am BMO the Brave and today the orders being given are mine, smart guy!"

Jake shrugs. "Okay."

A split second later, Jake transforms into a tiny little hot dog. And a split second *after that,* the Wormenstein slithers over and—*scarf!*—swallows Jake whole.

Finn's eyes go wide. "Holy Schmow! That Wormenstein just lumping *ate* Jake. BMO, what did you do?!"

"I guess it was a bad strategy," BMO says softly.

THE END

TWO?

Brain Teaser Bill's skull pops back onto his neck and all his old gray bones reassemble. "Ah, bones!" Brain Teaser Bill cries out in frustration. "You got it!"

BMO grins. "Now we will pass, I think."

Brain Teaser Bill kicks at the dirt. "Well, I guess I have to let you go now, don't I?"

"Good day, sir," Peppermint Butler says.

★ ✷ **BMO earns 13 ADVENTURE MINUTES.** ★ ✷

Keep on moving! Death is just around the corner.
TURN TO PAGE 114

LET'S DANCE, KITTEN!

Me-Mow spins around. An evil grin crosses the kitten's face. "Bite it, bot!" Me-Mow shouts. Me-Mow has a high-pitched voice and sounds like a five-year-old girl. It would be all sorts of adorable if the kitten weren't so lethal.

Me-Mow sprints up the side of a tree, out onto the branch, leaps—*she soars through the air*—and lands a vicious kick to BMO's face!

BMO cries out and stumbles back. "You have caused me much anger," the tiny robot growls.

BMO's hands ball up into tiny robot fists and BMO starts *launching haymakers*. Close, but no stogie! Me-Mow backflips away and dashes up a thin vine. The cat coughs but doesn't bring up a fur ball—she brings up a poisoned syringe!

"BMO, watch out!" Jake shouts.

BMO turns and—*POW!*—Me-Mow is swinging in on the vine! Me-Mow lands a tiny cat punch to BMO's screen! BMO stumbles back and lands in the grass.

The killer kitten is dancing on BMO's chest, spinning the needle. "Ready to get poked?" Me-Mow hisses.

BMO has one chance to land a punch and knock the evil assassin out for good. But BMO's vision is funky—that paw punch did some damage! BMO tries to focus, but the tiny robot is seeing double—no, *triple!*

HELP BMO DEFEAT ME-MOW!

There are three Me-Mow images below, but one is slightly different than the others. The one that's **different** is the real Me-Mow.

If you think the **first** Me-Mow is the *real* Me-Mow,
TURN TO PAGE 8

If you think the **second** Me-Mow is the *real* Me-Mow,
TURN TO PAGE 50

If you think the **third** Me-Mow is the *real* Me-Mow,
TURN TO PAGE 60

45

INTO THE
dREAM

BMO peers around the corner.

Yep, there he is: the King Worm. The giant green villain is at the foot of Princess Bubblegum's bed, lying perfectly still, being a big weird creep. PB is asleep on the bed, breathing softly and gently. Finn was right; the King Worm *totally* has her hypnotized!

"I need to get into her dream so I can wake her up!" BMO thinks.

BMO tiptoes into the room and past the King Worm. Princess Bubblegum's hand is hanging off the side of the bed. BMO takes hold of it.

"Bedtime for BMOs . . ." BMO whispers.

There is a tiny button on BMO's case. It reads: SLEEP. BMO reaches around and presses that tiny button and is quickly off to join PB in dreamland . . .

BMO wakes up *inside PB's dream*, and it is total lumping *DREAM WEIRDNESS!*

In the dream world, the bed is empty and the Princess is gone. But—*argh*—the King Worm is still keeping watch. BMO sneaks past the King Worm and out into the long castle hallway. The hallway twists and turns and spirals like a funky waterslide!

Why are dreams so weird?

46

BMO says aloud, "You are snoozing BMO, do not forget it or you will go batty!"

BMO takes another step and looks down. Gum! Gum beneath BMO's feet! BMO's eyes go wide—a trail of wet, sticky bubblegum lumps stretches down the hallway. It's like Princess Bubblegum is *melting* or something.

BMO takes off running, following the trail of lumps.

The castle is *superbizarre*—it's less like a dream and more like a nightmare. Eyes in the walls watch BMO run down the hallway. The floor is wet, like a chocolate river.

BMO turns the corner into the castle kitchen and finds Princess Bubblegum sitting on the floor, playing with a dollhouse. And the dolls are Finn and Jake! They're way tiny, the size of fingers!

Princess Bubblegum looks up at BMO. Her face is young! Even younger than Finn's! It's like the time the Ice King froze PB and she got all shattered and there wasn't enough bubblegum to put her back together, so she was stuck at age thirteen! "That's why her pink bubblegum stuff was everywhere!" BMO realizes. "She's, like, losing her body and getting younger!"

"Hi, BMO!" Princess Bubblegum says.

BMO says, "Princess, do you know you're in a dream?"

"I'm not in a dream!" Princess Bubblegum shoots back. "*You're in a dream!*"

"Yes I am." BMO smiles. "*Yours.*"

Princess Bubblegum just scowls and goes back to playing with the weird little Jake and Finn dolls. BMO needs to snap PB out of this dream before the King Worm knows what's going on!

"Princess, we need to defeat the King Worm!" BMO says.

"I don't want to defeat anything," Princess Bubblegum whines. "I just want to be *young* and *carefree!* What I wouldn't give to just let my hair down . . . like Finn!"

BMO is confused. "Finn wears a hat most of the time."

"Nah-uh! Look beneath your butt," Princess says.

BMO looks down and—*whoa!*—the hallway is turning golden yellow! The hallway, BMO realizes, is made *entirely* of hair! *Finn's hair.* It's like a spaghetti river of blond Finn hair rushing beneath BMO's feet.

Again, why are dreams so weird?!?!

"Princess, you are not a child," BMO shouts. "You need to wake up!"

Princess Bubblegum sticks her tongue out and scrunches her face up all funny. "Have to catch me first, BMO!"

And with that, Princess Bubblegum takes off, running through the maze of Finn hair . . .

HELP BMO CATCH UP TO PRINCESS BUBBLEGUM

Follow BMO into the maze of Finn hair. But be careful, once you pick a path, there's no turning back!

If you ended up at Princess Bubblegum, **TURN TO 71**

If you ended up at the sandbox, **TURN TO PAGE 7**

THE REAL
ME-MOW!

BMO focuses on the middle Me-Mow and *punches!*
KA-POW!

A direct hit to the killer kitten's nose. BMO chose correctly!
Party!

Me-Mow stumbles back. Her eyes cross and she collapses.
The killer kitty is out cold!

"I showed you, Me-Mow!" Jake shouts.

"Actually, I think BMO showed her. Way to go BMO!"
Finn exclaims.

BMO is very proud. The little robot's tiny hands brush
together. "All in a day's work for BMO the Brave."

Jake is still rubbing his head where Me-Mow whomped
him. "Yeah, thanks BMO. That kitten
had us busted up pretty good."

BMO smiles and asks, "I can come for
the rest of the adventure?"

Finn grins. "Yes, BMO, you can
come."

"Woo-hoo!"

The trio splits before the killer cat
wakes up from her BMO-induced
slumber. They take off into

the woods—Finn running, Jake following, and BMO just trying to keep up.

BMO is grinning wildly—BMO is a hero!

But the true adventure is just beginning . . .

★ ✹ **BMO** earns 15 ADVENTURE MINUTES. ★ ★

To continue this action-packed adventure,
TURN TO PAGE 16

WEDDING AVERTED

"What? Are you lumping serious?!" LSP cries out.

"It is true. He does not love you for your lumps. The recording proves it!"

The Earl of Lemongrab starts sweating. He's definitely about to *go big-time ballistic*. He screams at the top of his lungs! *AHHHH!*

And then he *runs*—straight out the front door, headed back to Castle Lemongrab.

"*What the lump!?*" LSP screams. "I wanted to get married!"

Marceline grins. "Nice work, BMO. Just wait until Finn and Jake hear about your butt-kicking adventure."

BMO grins proudly. "It is all in a day's work for the hero, BMO!"

"More like BMO the jerk wedding ruiner . . ." LSP huffs.

★ ★ **BMO earns 50 ADVENTURE MINUTES.** ★ ★

THE END

ROCK MONSTERS DON'T ROCK

"I can see the portal!" Finn shouts. "Kick-butt navigating, BMO!"

The portal glows at the end of the path—but getting there is not going to be easy! Skeletons lunge and grab at the friends. And then, something worse than any old skeleton—

All of a sudden, blocking the path, is a towering beast of stone! A *rock* monster. Dozens of small rocks combine to form one massive creature.

BMO slides to a stop—Finn slams into BMO, and Jake slams into Finn. "What's the holdup?" Jake shouts.

"The giant rock monster," Finn says. "That's the holdup!"

"Oh. I see."

BMO's mind is racing. The creature is made up of a whole *butt-ton* of rocks. If they can knock out one, maybe the whole monster will collapse!

But how to knock out one?

"Jake can break the rocks!" BMO realizes.

"Huh? I can?" Jake asks.

"Yes. Get rubberized and weave in between them—you can separate them!"

Jake shrugs. "Okay, dudes, I'll try . . ."

★ ★ **BMO earns 35 ADVENTURE MINUTES.** ★ ★

FOLLOW JAKE'S RUBBER ARMS TO DEFEAT THE GIANT ROCK MONSTER!

Guide Jake's *two arms* through the creature's cracks
and crevices. Each time Jake's hands cross, Jake gives
himself a thunderous Jake-to-Jake power slap. Enough
power slaps and he'll break the monster apart!
Mark down the number of times his hands cross in
the box on the next page.

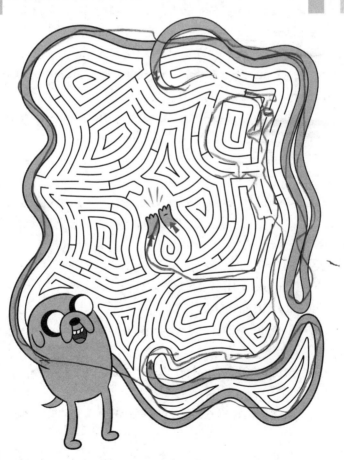

54

Jake-to-Jake power slaps

TOTAL:

If Jake gives himself 1-4 power slaps,
TURN TO PAGE 53

If Jake gives himself 5+ power slaps,
TURN TO PAGE 27

A BRIEF STOP IN THE ICE KINGDOM

BMO and Marceline pass through the green grasslands and into the chilled-out Ice Kingdom. They march over snowy hills and across icy plains. In the distance are hundreds of pointy mountains—the largest, pointiest mountain is the castle of that miserable babe chaser, the Ice King.

BMO is slipping and sliding on the ice, so Marceline scoops the tiny robot up, and together they float along. "So, Marceline, whose wedding are we going to stop?" BMO asks.

Marceline is about to answer when a figure appears, blocking their path. Marceline moans. "Oh, crudders."

Oh, crudders is right. It's the Ice King! He flies high above Marceline and BMO, his beard flapping.

"A wedding!" the Ice King exclaims. "Did someone say wedding!? Whose wedding!?"

Marceline sets BMO down and rolls her eyes. "This isn't a good time, Simon."

"I want to go to a wedding!" the Ice King exclaims. "Weddings are a great place to meet princess babes. All of those maids of honor. Heh, more like *babes of honor*. Am I right?"

BMO frowns. This is an adventure, and they can't have the Ice King tagging along. He'll muck it all up. And he's a villain! Villains don't join heroes on adventures. He'll totally kidnap a princess or lose his mind or blast someone with ice bolts or some junk.

BMO knows that the Ice King can not—*no way, no how*—tag along. So BMO says, "Ice King, you can not—*no way, no how*—tag along."

The Ice King's beard stops flapping and he lands. "Hey now! This is my kingdom and I'll do whatever I want!"

"Ice King . . . *be nice,*" Marceline warns.

"What? I'm always nice. Except when I'm chasing *the ladies.* Do Finn and Jake not think I'm nice? Is that why they never want to hang out?"

Marceline rolls her eyes so far they almost pop out of her head. BMO watches her, then does the same thing.

"Hey, c'mon, don't roll your eyes at me!" The Ice King pouts, "I'm tired of ladies rolling their eyes at me."

Marceline takes BMO's tiny hand in hers. "Okay, Ice King. Whatever. We're leaving now."

"*NO!*" the Ice King roars. "No, no, no! You are trespassing. That is the only rule in the Ice Kingdom: no trespassing! If you want to get through, Marceline, you need to pay the toll."

"What toll?"

Whoops. Now the Ice King is confused. He scratches his head. "Oh right. '*What toll?*' It sounded like a good idea, you know, '*just pay a toll.*' Hmm . . . need to think about this some."

Marceline taps her foot. BMO does the same. The Ice King feels their eyes upon him, waiting for him to make a decision.

"Um, um, um," the Ice King stammers, then finally exclaims, "The BMO toll!"

Marceline and BMO exchange worried glances.

"I'm sick of being surrounded by Gunters," the Ice King continues. "I could use some BMO action round here. Little change of pace."

"This is just silly," Marceline says and tries to brush past the Ice King.

"No. Marceline, you SHALL NOT PASS!" the Ice King roars. Alas, the roar was a regrettable move. Everyone knows you can't roar when you're surrounded by snowy mountains! Stupid Ice King . . .

There's a deafening rumble! Snow is tumbling toward them! It's an avalanche! And inside the avalanche is what looks like tiny black dots being tossed.

BMO's eyes narrow.

The black dots are Gunters! There are like *a hundred* tiny penguins, rolling down the mountain! One nearly knocks the Ice King off his feet! Another lands—SMACK!—in a tree.

Marceline yanks BMO off the ground and they hover high in the air so that the avalanche tumbles beneath them.

Finally, the snow settles. The Ice King is way perplexed. "What happened? Oh . . . Oh no . . . Gunters everywhere. BMO, Marceline, please, help me find all the Gunters!"

BMO smiles slyly. "We would love to help you, Ice King. But what about the BMO toll?"

The Ice King scowls. "Fine! If you help me find **all** the Gunters, you can *both* pass. Okay? Can you help?"

CAN YOU KEEP BMO FROM BECOMING THE ICE KING'S PRISONER?

How many Gunters do you see hiding in this picture?
Count them all.

If you spy 15 Gunters, **TURN TO PAGE 94**

If you spy 8 Gunters, **TURN TO PAGE 61**

RIGHT IS WRONG!

BMO launches a punch at the Me-Mow on the far right. But that's not the real Me-Mow!

BMO *whiffs*, and the momentum carries the tiny robot to the ground.

BMO stands up, very embarrassed and spitting out leaves.

Me-Mow spins the syringe, ready to attack.

All of a sudden, BMO is not feeling so superbrave. Does BMO not have the soul of a true hero? BMO has some serious thinking to do. With Finn, Jake, and Me-Mow all watching, BMO turns and runs, headed back to the Tree Fort . . .

Before BMO can be a hero, BMO needs a hero's soul . . .

★ ★ **BMO earns 2 ADVENTURE MINUTES.** ★ ★

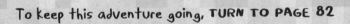

To keep this adventure going, TURN TO PAGE 82

A LOVELY DATE

The Ice King looks around and counts the Gunters. "Five, six, seven, and—"

The Ice King spins back around and pokes BMO. "Wrong!" he shouts. The Ice King is giddy now, hopping from foot to foot.

"Let's go, BMO," the Ice King says, grabbing BMO's hand and tugging the tiny robot toward the Ice Castle.

"Don't stress, BMO!" Marceline shouts. "I'll get Jake and Finn, and we'll come back for you!"

BMO throws one last glance at Marceline. BMO has never felt so miserable . . .

★ ✹ ✶

A little while later—not a short time but also not a crazy long time—BMO is in the Ice King's throne room. A supercute little frown is displayed on BMO's screen.

The Ice King has his legs crossed, trying to look very sophisticated—but he's failing, because the Ice King is a lame-o. "So BMO, do you like flowers?" the Ice King asks.

BMO shrugs. "Okay," BMO says.

The Ice King shoves a pair of flowers in BMO's face. "Good! Enjoy these flowers!"

BMO sulks. The ice chamber echoes with the most awkward of awkward silences. The Ice King coughs into his hand and says, "Finally, alone. Am I right?"

BMO sighs.

More awkward silence fills the room.

The Ice King beams as his heart pounds in his chest. "This is a wonderful date."

THE END

ENTRANCE
DENIED!

"That . . . is . . . incorrect . . ." the frog says.

"No!" Marceline exclaims.

"The . . . portal . . . is . . . closed . . . to . . . you . . ." the frog says, *"FOREVER . . ."*

Marceline glares at BMO. BMO's guess at the password failed! Now, the future of Land of Ooo is in jeopardy.

THE END

FAILED
ESCAPE!

The Banana Guards rub their eyes as the flash dims! But then, one shrieks! As they examine themselves, they realize the key to the dungeon is missing! "The key! That tiny robot stole it!"

The Banana Guard looks down to see BMO escaping from the jail.

"Halt!" the Banana Guard cries.

BMO is running as fast as robotically possible! But before the tiny robot can make it to freedom, *the King Worm slithers in!*

"It seems we'll need to double the guards," the King Worm says.

Now BMO will never be able to rescue Princess Bubblegum! And now *everyone* is trapped in the dungeon *forever.*

THE END

BMO BEHIND THE WHEEL

BMO grins and says, "Trust me, Melissa. I am all over this situation. I am an expert high-speed-chase driver."

Melissa sighs. "Fine."

The ladies hop into the car, and BMO puts the pedal to the metal!

HELP BMO GET TO THE WEDDING!

On the next page, start at the arrow. You can move up, down, left, or right. You may not move diagonally, and you may not cross the same pattern more than twice.

If you get stuck, go back to the beginning and start again!

If you finish at the tree, **TURN TO PAGE 68**
If you finish at LSP, **TURN TO PAGE 99**

BACK INTO
DEATH'S ARMS

"I don't think this is right, guys!" Jake shouts.

And Jake is right . . . They're looping back around, past the skeletons, and into the arms of Death.

Death grins. "Now, I will take *ALL OF YOUR SOULS!*"

"Ah, c'mon," Jake moans.

"BMO, I told you not to go on an adventure!" Finn cries out.

And that's that . . .

THE END

FENDER
BENDER

"BMO, watch out for that tree!" Marceline shouts.

"Oh my glob!" Melissa screams. "We're all going to lumping die!"

Marceline, since she's a radical vampire and radical vampires can fly, grabs hold of BMO and glides out of the car just as it *SLAMS* into a tree.

BMO stumbles around to the front of the car to peep the damage. "It appears I may have overestimated my driving skills," BMO says.

Suddenly, the sound of church bells—a big, loud, epic *dong, dong, dong*—travels across the lumpy abyss and through the lumpy skies. It can only mean one thing—the wedding is about to begin!

"Oh my glob!" Melissa cries out. "We have to hurry!"

But there's a major lumping issue. Melissa's car is smoking like Saturday barbeque! The front is all dented up and junk, and the lumpy space engine is big-time busted.

Marceline frowns and crosses her arms. "BMO, any chance you know how to fix a crumpled lumpy space car?"

"I can try . . ."

HELP BMO FIX THE ENGINE!

Can you trace all the engine wires in a single continuous line, without going back over any of the lines you've already drawn and without lifting your pencil from the page?

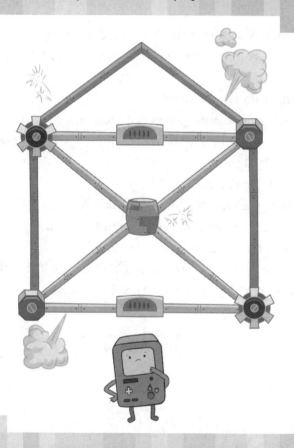

If you can do it, **TURN TO PAGE 99**

If you don't think it's possible, **TURN TO PAGE 13**

REBOOT

BMO's screen flashes three times, but the tiny robot never even moves. Marceline is heartbroken. "Oh no . . . BMO . . . I'm so sorry . . ."

But, suddenly, BMO sits up!

"Whoa! Kick-butt!" Marceline exclaims.

BMO grins. But it's a weird grin . . . a little creepy . . . "Hello," BMO says.

"BMO, you're okay!"

"Who is BMO?" the tiny robot asks.

"Um . . . you are," Marceline says, confused.

"I am sorry. I do not know any BMO."

Oh no . . . BMO's memory has been wiped! The real, true, *awesome and lovable* BMO has been lost forever . . .

THE END

DESTROY
THE DREAMSCAPE!

BMO *bursts* out of the strange maze of hair and—*whoa*—BMO is standing on top of a giant, football field–sized version of Finn's forehead! **Weirdest. Dream. Ever.**

"Please . . . Get . . . Off . . . My . . . Cranium . . ." the giant Finn bellows.

"I am apologizing, Finn!" BMO says. Up ahead, Princess Bubblegum is sprinting around Finn's mouth. BMO gives chase across the giant Finn face, finally tackling the princess from behind.

"You got me!" Princess Bubblegum giggles.

BMO jumps up and, superquick, the tiny robot's screen changes so that it now shows an image of the *real*, normal, nondream Princess Bubblegum. "Look, Princess! This is the true you!" BMO says.

Princess Bubblegum's eyes go wide. She stares at the screen. "Oh my—"

"See! Remember? Right now, you're in a dream!" BMO says. "The King Worm put you in a sleepy-time trance. We need to *destroy* the dream so you can have wake-ups!"

"Okay," Princess Bubblegum says, thinking hard. After a moment she hollers, "Um . . . *DESTROY DREAM!*"

Nothing happens.

Neither of them move—waiting, hoping . . .

Nope. Nothing.

Suddenly, a voice echoes throughout the dream kingdom. *"Hey there. Why are you doing that?"*

Uh-oh. It's *the King Worm*, in the dream! The creature is inching his way across Finn's giant forehead.

Suddenly, Finn's giant mouth opens and begins talking. "Don't worry, buddies. Just beat up the King Worm inside the dream and that'll make him lose his grip on you. Easy peasy."

BMO and Princess Bubblegum exchange glances. "Okay, seems easy enough."

"Sorry, guys. Not so easy peasy. I can't let you do that," the King Worm says. And with that, the ground beneath BMO—*that's Finn's face!*—changes into thousands of tiny green worms, crawling *all over* BMO!

"Please get off me!" BMO cries, thrashing at the worms. "Princess, help me! It's not my dream so I can't do cool magic stuff!"

"Oh right," the Princess says. "Okay. Umm . . . *BMO—GET BIG!*"

It works! BMO is transforming—becoming GIANT-SIZED BMO! BMO's tiny legs and tiny body multiply by ten! BMO is the size of King Worm! All the tiny worms fall from Giant-Sized BMO's giant-sized body.

Now BMO can be more than a hero, BMO can be a *dream hero*. "I don't like you, King Worm!" Giant-Sized BMO shouts. "And I'm going to hurt you!"

Giant-Sized BMO *charges* the King Worm and *punches*. **POW!** The worm's big, green lollipop head falls to the side.

Giant-Sized BMO lands another blow, and the entire dream world shakes!

"It's working!" Giant-Sized BMO cries out.

Giant-Sized BMO head-butts the King Worm. The King Worm stumbles back. With every blow, the dream world cracks and the King Worm grows weaker.

Giant-Sized BMO *body slams* the worm and the ground beneath their feet disappears! The sky shatters! The King Worm is almost defeated! He is now just a wrinkled husk of a creature.

BMO lands one final punch—a killer BMO uppercut! And the dream world breaks apart! Green light shoots out of the King Worm's head in every direction! Everything crumbles! The sky falls away!

And just like that, the dream is over . . .

BMO is back inside the bedroom, standing next to Princess Bubblegum, *BACK IN THE REAL WORLD!*

BMO is normal sized and awake and Princess Bubblegum is back to her real age. She sits up in the bed, looking dazed and confused. "BMO, what happened?"

BMO collapses on the floor, exhausted. "It's a long story . . ."

"Whoa, is that the King Worm?" the princess says, pointing to his molted husk on the floor.

"Yes, that is the wormy villain."

"Wow," Princess Bubblegum says. "Wait, where are Finn and Jake?"

"You put them in the dungeon."

"I did?"

"Yes."

"Weird day."

"You have no idea, sister," BMO says with a grin.

★ ✶ **BMO** *earns* 50 ADVENTURE MINUTES. ★ ✶

THE END

THE WEDDING
GOES ON!

No! That's not what the recording says—and everyone knows it!

LSP frowns. "BMO, I don't believe that for *one lumping second*!"

The earl screams at BMO, "**Wrong!** You are wrong! I love this—um—ahh—beautiful lady! Let the wedding continue! **NOW! CONTINUE NOW!**"

And the wedding *does* continue. LSP and the Earl of Lemongrab are *married!* And now, all of Ooo is in jeopardy, 'cause *no one* knows what that nut cake will do with his newfound power.

BMO . . .

Has . . .

Failed . . .

THE END

SOUL
SEARCHING

BMO waddles through the Tree Fort and into the bathroom and climbs up onto the sink. BMO spins the faucet knobs and turns on the hot water. Soon, the room is steaming like pasta breakfast.

BMO stares deeply into the mirror, feeling super self-inquiring and junk.

"I want to be a real boy!" BMO exclaims.

But how do I become a real boy?

"I need a soul!" BMO realizes.

But where do I get my own personal BMO soul?

"I don't know." BMO shrugs.

Maybe if you just ask.

"Ask who?" BMO wonders.

Ask the world!

BMO's inner thoughts are kind of freaking the little robot out. But what was there to lose? So . . .

"I want a boy's soul!" BMO announces to the world.

Nothing happens.

Hmm . . .

But wait! What's that?

In the mirror, BMO can see someone climbing through the window and into the bathroom! But through the steam, BMO isn't 100 percent supersure who it is . . .

HELP BMO FIGURE OUT WHO'S CLIMBING THROUGH THE WINDOW

Shade in the shapes with an odd number of sides to reveal the identity of the snoop in the window.

If you think it's Tree Trunks, **TURN TO PAGE 108**

If you think it's Peppermint Butler,
TURN TO PAGE 110

ATTaCk
PB!

"Attack PB!" BMO shouts. "It is our only hope of conquest!"

Finn and BMO leap to the ground as Jake transforms back into his usual awesome self. Finn and Jake march toward the possessed and deranged Princess Bubblegum.

But, alas, Finn and Jake cannot fight the princess . . .

Finn wants to whip out his razor-sharp sword, but he can't! He could never attack PB!

Finn drops his sword. Princess Bubblegum smiles triumphantly. "Jake, Finn, BMO," Princess Bubblegum says. "Please meet my new friend, the King Worm."

Oh. Crud.

To meet the monster that has control over Princess Bubblegum, TURN TO PAGE 40

INTO THE LAND
OF THE DEAD

BMO steps through.

The portal disappears with a *zap*, leaving BMO and Peppermint Butler standing on a chunk of cold, floating rock high above the Land of the Dead.

BMO is absolutely *terrified*.

"Don't worry," Peppermint Butler says, "I have friends here."

"Here?" BMO asks, not quite believing it.

"Indeed. Now follow me," Peppermint Butler says, before— holy geez—*leaping* off the rock!

BMO doesn't want to jump. Not at all. But BMO *does* want to be a real boy. So—

BMO dives!

The tiny robot plummets through the Land of the Dead, the most terrifying place *not* on Earth. BMO rockets past jagged spikes and giant scorpions. Bloodred hands grab for BMO! Thousands of beady eyes watch BMO speed by while giant skulls with chattering teeth

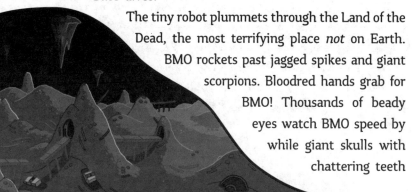

chomp and ghosts appear and disappear in puffs of ghostly smoke!

BMO continues plummeting down, down, down into the Land of the Dead.

"I'm going to crash and break!" BMO cries out.

But just then, a giant, skeletal hawk swoops down. BMO and Peppermint Butler land on the back of the big, bony bird and BMO hangs on for dear life as the hawk swoops toward the ground.

The hawk lands and BMO hops off ultraquick, thinking maybe this adventure has gotten out of hand. But still, the desire for a soul calls to the tiny robot . . .

BMO looks around. The sky is shadowy and endless. In one direction are great plains. In the other is a deep, dark canyon.

"Which way do we go?" BMO asks Peppermint Butler.

DECODE THE MESSAGE TO LEARN WHICH WAY PEP-BUT THINKS THEY SHOULD GO.

Look at the scrambled message below. Cross out all the letters that appear in the word **PEP-BUT**—the remaining letters will tell you whether Pep-But thinks they should travel through the canyon or across the plains. Then it's up to you to decide whether BMO should listen to Pep-But or not!

PTCEAUNBYTOUNPE

If you agree with Pep-But, **TURN TO PAGE 85**

If you disagree, **TURN TO PAGE 114**

BMO
GOES SOLO

BMO opens the door and steps outside. The grass is green and the sky is blue and the sun is big and bright in the sky. It is a totally perfect day for a kick-butt adventure!

"They can have their no-BMOs-allowed adventure," BMO thinks. "I'll have my own personal adventure that is only for awesome BMOs."

But where to find that adventure? That's always the first question one must ask when setting out for some old-school adventuring.

But just then, at that moment, the adventure comes to BMO . . . The sky darkens like lumping thunderstorm town. A figure is flying toward BMO, blocking out the sun.

It's Marceline!

The pale-white and punky vampire queen is sporting dark pants with radical rips in them and a bloodred T-shirt, and she's holding a big sun umbrella over her head—per the usual, she's looking wicked and bodacious.

"Hey, BMO," Marceline says as she lands. "Are Finn and Jake around?"

BMO ponders the situation. Marceline is probably going to grab Finn and Jake and whisk them off on some exciting exploit. But that should be BMO's exciting exploit! Hmm . . . Inside BMO's robot mind, a plan is forming—and BMO needs to play it cool. But that's no problem, playing it cool is BMO's specialty . . .

"Have you ever *met* Finn and Jake?" BMO asks slyly.

Marceline lands and sighs. "BMO, don't be weird, I'm in a rush. I need Finn and Jake. It's crazy important."

BMO continues to play dumb. "I do not know this Finn and Jake," BMO says. "You must mean *Finnyjake*, the famous tiny robot adventurer. Yes, that is me. *Finnyjake*."

Marceline puts her hands on her hips and cocks her head. "BMO, don't make me transform and freak you out. 'Cause I will. I need Finn and Jake, *right now.*"

BMO's digital display transforms into a frown. "I am apologetic, but I do not know this BMO character. But I can aid you! I will join whatever adventure you have that needs joining!"

BMO expects a very dramatic response from Marceline, but instead—

"Ah, fine," Marceline says with a shrug. "Let's go. But listen, I'm *not* calling you Finnyjake. I'm calling you BMO, 'cause that's your name. You dig?"

"Superfantastic!" BMO says. "Now, where are we are going?"

"To stop a wedding and help a friend and save the Land of Ooo. No biggie."

★ ★ **BMO earns 6 ADVENTURE MINUTES.** ★ ★

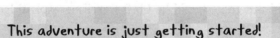

This adventure is just getting started!
TURN TO PAGE 56

THROUGH
THE CANYON

BMO and Pep-But have been walking for hours when they come across *the weirdest thing BMO has ever seen!* It is: **a giant brain!** It's a massive pink blob as big as a house. And it's *alive.* Surrounding the brain are skeleton people, dancing around and pelting it with rocks.

They're teasing the poor pink thing, BMO realizes.

One of the skeletons calls out, "Hey, brain, you smell! You smell like musty old brain stuff!"

Another skeleton throws a rock and shouts, "Nice catch, brain! *Not!*"

"What are those guys? BMO asks.

"Brain teasers . . ." Peppermint Butler says. "They're a cruel kind of skeleton person. Bullies . . ."

The brain slinks away, dragging its brainy body across the cold ground and leaving a path of pink slime behind it. That's when one of the brain teasers spots BMO and Peppermint Butler.

"Hey, where do you think you're going?" the brain teaser demands.

"I'm looking for a boy's soul," BMO says.

"Then you've come to the right place! I'm Brain Teaser Bill. What are you, like a little robot or something? That's pretty cool." Brain Teaser Bill has a big smile on his bony face and a friendly voice, but BMO knows he's just a cruel and callous ole bully.

Brain Teaser Bill squeezes BMO's tiny arms. "No meat on your little robot bones, huh?"

"No," BMO squeaks.

"That's a good thing for you, otherwise I'd eat you!" Brain Teaser Bill says.

"Just point us in the direction of Death," Peppermint Butler demands.

Brain Teaser Bill thinks for a moment, then says, "Sorry, no. I think I'd rather take this little robot's soul. Death will be *very* excited if I bring him a little *robot soul.*"

Peppermint Butler toddles forward. "I am a *personal friend* of Death's. You will be in serious trouble if you do not let my friend and I pass."

The Brain Teaser frowns. "Hmm . . . Well, I don't want to get in trouble with the big guy. But I can't just let you pass, either, I'm a Brain Teaser! It'd ruin my rep. So here, solve one of my *brain teasers,* and you may go on your way."

Suddenly, Brain Teaser Bill collapses in a heap of bones! But he keeps talking—the big jaw on his skull keeps yapping away. "Okay," Brain Teaser Bill says, "get ready to be *teased* by this Brain Teaser!"

HELP BMO SOLVE THE BRAIN TEASER'S BRAIN TEASER

See these four squares made up of twelve bones? Brain Teaser Bill wants BMO to remove bones, one by one, until *only two squares remain*. What is the *least* amount of bones you can remove to turn these four squares into two squares?

If you think the answer is 2, **TURN TO PAGE 43**

If you think the answer is 4, **TURN TO PAGE 88**

FOUR?

"Wrong!" Brain Teaser Bill says as his skeleton reassembles.

Brain Teaser Bill begins preparing BMO's soul for extraction. But the skeleton is confused! It's not working! "Hey! Wait . . . Why can I not have your soul!? What's wrong here?" Brain Teaser Bill says.

BMO grins. "It seems that I, BMO, have *teased* the *brain teaser.* Robots do not have souls."

"Ahh, you tricked me! You tricked the tricker!" Brain Teaser Bill pouts.

"That is just how I roll," BMO says.

And with that, BMO and Peppermint Butler journey on, leaving behind a very unfulfilled Brain Teaser Bill.

★ ✹ **BMO earns 11 ADVENTURE MINUTES.** ★ ✹

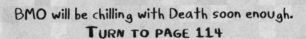

BMO will be chilling with Death soon enough.
TURN TO PAGE 114

ATTaCk FAILs!

No! One thunderous Jake Clap too few! Jake knocks out the creature's knees, but not the rest!

And knocking out the knees is bad news . . .

The massive monster is falling! Tumbling down on top of the gang!

"Finn, I love you, man," Jake says.

"I know," Finn responds.

BMO's tiny eyes shut tight . . .

KRUNCH!

THE END

JAKE WORM, YO!

"You will become Jake Worm!" BMO declares.

Finn grins. "I **love** that plan!"

"Jack Worm, yo." Jake nods. "Jake Worm."

It is agreed—

JAKE WORM!

With superquickness, Jake begins morphing and stretching into a giant worm. He is now Jake Worm and he is as big as the Wormenstein! Jake flicks his fat worm tail and sends BMO and Finn cartwheeling through the air and up onto his back.

BMO scrambles up on top of Jake's wormy head and points at the Wormenstein. "Full-steam ahead, Jake Worm!"

"Um, you can just call me Jake, still," Jake says.

"No! Jake Worm!" BMO declares.

Jake sighs.

Jake—er, *Jake Worm*—does a radical worm impersonation and slithers forward.

"Watch out, guys!" Finn shouts to the Candy People below, and they all go running and diving and ducking and hiding.

The gargantuan Wormenstein is slithering forward toward Jake Worm, putting the two monstrosities on a collision course! It's about to be a total clash of the worm titans outside the castle walls.

94

Finn and BMO hang on tight as the two massive worm creatures **collide!** An epic wet, mushy sound echoes across the land. It's gross.

Jake Worm and the Wormenstein began brawling.

Only problem?

Worms don't really have *arms,* so Jake Worm and the Wormenstein are sort of just rubbing against each other, nuzzling like puppies. Jake cranes his big worm neck to look back to BMO and Finn. "Guys, this is awkward. All these little worms are, like, crawling all over me and touching me. Honest opinion? Jake Worm stinks for fighting."

"Jake Worm, you do not talk, you battle!" BMO says.

"I can't! I think you need to adjust your plan, BMO!" Jake shouts.

★ ★ **BMO earns 26 ADVENTURE MINUTES.** ★ ★

HELP BMO FIGURE OUT A NEW PLAN!

Many *Adventure Time* locations are hidden in the word search on the next page. How many can you find? They can be across, up, down, diagonal, or even backward.

```
V F Y G H F B T K I J R E C P L
E C D I C E K I N G D O M O R E
R G A D Q R O B P X H N I T Q P
D B E S V R Y Q R I H O M T H M
A L D D T B G E N F K R M O O A
N K E O R L M B I A N Y M N M H
T T H C E U E E F R S N J C Y C
P E T A T B R L L T M T E A A F
L L F P R J J U E J T C C N X U
A E O Q O D G R M M A A D D D X
I K D F F U Y U O P O Y G Y G E
N X N S E T L I S K K N F F W Y
U L A A E Z C Y G I T V G O L B
C A L M R O P D N F W J A R Z A
R N P G T M K G A G D R C E A O
A L B I U N D F N S J E C S U B
E B T L V O A T M C L I M T N N
X C R O M C A N D Y T A V E R N
```

If you find 1-5 words, **TURN TO PAGE 35**

If you find 6-10 words, **TURN TO PAGE 78**

VICTORY
FOR DEATH!

"Yeahhhhh!" Death screams. "*Finally!*"

BMO grins. "Yes, Mr. Death! You won the game!"

Death stands up and dusts himself off. "But now we have a problem, little robot."

Uh-oh, BMO thinks. "We do?"

Death nods. "We do. That game is way fun. Too fun. I'm not sure I can live—and I use the term 'live,' loosely, of course—without it. You can have your soul—any soul you want! But, yeah . . . I can never allow you to leave here."

So that's that . . .

BMO will get the soul that it so badly craved. But BMO—soul and all—will now be forced to live for all eternity as Death's personal video-game system . . .

THE END

PEACE OUT,
ICE KING!

"Aww, stank pants!" the Ice King moans. "You're right . . ."

Marceline pats BMO on the back. "Way to count, BMO."

BMO grins and leans over and whispers to Marceline, "I think we should go before he does the freak-out."

With that, Marceline scoops up BMO and whisks the tiny robot away, leaving the Ice King to "do the freak-out."

Marceline and BMO cross through the Ice Kingdom, journey past the strange Mystery Temple, then finally come to the beautiful Verdant Plains. The grass is very high and BMO can barely see through it. BMO is getting frustrated. "Marceline, I think you should tell me where we are going and what this adventure is."

"It's crazy bad beans, BMO. Lumpy Space Princess—" Marceline begins, before pausing for dramatic effect.

"What?" BMO asks. "What *about* Lumpy Space Princess?!"

"Lumpy Space Princess . . ." Marceline continues, "*IS GETTING MARRIED!*"

BMO moans. "That's not a type of adventure!"

"You don't understand. She's going to marry that psycho, the Earl of Lemongrab."

"Lumpy Space Princess can marry whoever she wants," BMO says. "That's what I reason."

Marceline scowls. "The Earl of Lemongrab is only marrying her so he can become Prince of Lumpy Space and have *two kingdoms*. That'll make it crazy easy for him to take over the whole lumping Land of Ooo!"

"Oh," BMO says softly. BMO thinks about this for a moment, then declares, "We shall go save the day as heroes!"

"Right on!"

Marceline whisks BMO through the grass and soon, in a clearing, they come upon a mushroom and a frog. "I think this is the place . . ." Marceline says.

Marceline looks down at the frog and asks "Hey, wart-breath, are you a portal?"

The frog goes *"Ribbit."*

"Knock it off, Frog. You're a portal, right?" Marceline says.

Again, the frog is just all, like, *"Ribbit."*

BMO steps forward. "Hello, Frog. Are you a portal to Lumpy Space? This person needs help," BMO says. BMO's screen changes to show an image of Lumpy Space Princess.

Finally, *at last*, the frog opens his mouth and says something besides *ribbit*. The frog says: "Password, please."

"I don't know any silly password," Marceline says.

BMO steps forward. "Mr. Frog, this is extra urgent. The future of Ooo depends on us!"

"You . . . cannot . . . enter . . .without . . .the . . . password . . ." the frog says, "But . . . if . . . you . . . really . . . know . . . her . . . you . . . would . . . have . . . read . . . that . . . utterly . . . horrible . . . paperback . . . she . . . authored . . ."

Huh? BMO is confused . . . That's a weird thing for the frog to say.

But then BMO realizes it! The frog is trying to help them! The name of LSP's book—*that* must be the password!

HELP BMO FIGURE OUT THE PASSWORD

BMO is able to turn the frog's words into a clue! The frog said: If you really know her, you would have read that utterly horrible paperback she authored.

Find those words in the grid below, then cross them out. The leftover words are the password!

IF	REALLY	A	UTTERLY
I	PAPERBACK	READ	THAT
HORRIBLE	WROTE	HAVE	WOULD
AUTHORED	SHE	KNOW	BOOK

If you think the password is *I Wrote A Book*,
TURN TO PAGE 32

If you think the password is
That Utterly Horrible Paperback, **TURN TO PAGE 63**

96

DEATH IS A
TERRIBLE GAMER

"Ahh, c'mon!" Death shouts, slamming the controller into the ground with frustration.

BMO frowns. "Um, Mr. Death? I'd really just like to get my soul and go home now."

"You'll have your soul when I win!"

Yikes.

Peppermint Butler pipes up. "You guys have fun. I'm going to return to the Candy Kingdom."

"Later, buddy!" Death says, barely taking his eyes off the game.

Peppermint Butler trots off into the distance, leaving BMO behind . . .

As BMO has discovered, the king of the Land of the Dead is a serious berserker video-game *addict* and he refuses to stop until he wins!

Hours and hours and more hours pass.

BMO is beginning to realize there may only be two options here . . .

UNSCRAMBLE THE WORDS TO FIGURE OUT BMO'S TWO OPTIONS:

OPTION #1:

LTE TDAEH WNI

OPTION #2:

MAEK IHM AERN TI

If you think BMO should choose Option #1,
TURN TO PAGE 103

If you think BMO should choose Option #2,
TURN TO PAGE 109

STOP THE WEDDING!

Seventeen minutes later they pull up to the wedding, looking only slightly worse for the wear.

This wedding is like *the event* of the season. BMO sees lumpy limousines and Lumpy Space ladies in bright green and yellow dresses and Lumpy Space dudes in slick tuxedos and enormous spotlights shining into the sky.

BMO hops out of the car and runs toward the wedding chapel.

"BMO, are you sure you don't want my help or—" Marceline calls out.

"No! This is BMO's adventure!" BMO says.

BMO needs to find the Earl of Lemongrab *immediately* and put a stop to his plan. BMO sprints around the rear of the wedding chapel and jumps up, trying to peer through the window.

There!

BMO gets a glimpse of the Earl of Lemongrab. He's getting dressed and is looking pretty, *pretty* sharp in his fancy earl tuxedo.

"Okay BMO, it is action-hero time!"

BMO scales the side of the chapel like a mountain explorer and crawls through an open window and out onto a very thin wooden beam, overlooking the Earl of Lemongrab's room.

The earl stands in front of a mirror, telling himself how great he is. "You are smart! *SO SMART!*"

The Earl is definitely a superweirdo.

"My plan is perfect!" the earl continues.

"This is it!" BMO thinks. "He's gabbing about his plan. If I record him and play it for LSP, I can halt this nuptial!"

BMO is full of all sorts of mechanical gadgets, and one is a tape recorder. BMO steps to the edge of the wooden beam and begins recording . . .

The Earl of Lemongrab howls: "Once I marry that lumpy thing, I'll be prince of Lumpy Space. And I will be destined to rule TWO kingdoms! *TWO KINGDOMS!* My power will be unmatched! *UNMATCHED!*"

Got it!

This guy is busted like dropped dishes. All BMO needs to do is play that recording for LSP and the wedding will be off, and Ooo will be saved! BMO toddles back across the wooden beam, headed for the window. But—

KRAK!

Uh-oh. The chapel is way old . . . The beam beneath BMO's feet is breaking . . .

The Earl of Lemongrab hears the sound and looks up. "What?! *What are you doing?!*" he shrieks.

There's another *KRAK!* and the beam breaks! BMO tumbles to the floor.

"Who are you?!? *WHO ARE YOU!!?*" the earl cries. The earl is a supernut and he pretty much only communicates by screaming and yelling like a lunatic.

"I am BMO the Brave!" BMO says proudly. "And I have foiled your plot.

Now it is time for me to say see you later!"

With that, BMO sprints through the Earl of Lemongrab's window and out into the chapel. Everyone gasps! Gasps all around.

The Earl of Lemongrab charges after BMO, about to FREAK OUT. "This—*this*—*thing* was spying on me!" he shrieks.

LSP's father, sitting in the front row, stands up. "What is the meaning of this!?"

LSP, who is looking pretty rad in her supercute white wedding dress, flies forward. "BMO!" LSP cries. "What the *lump* are you doing?"

"LSP, I have the terrible news for you. You can not espouse this yellow jerk boss."

LSP's head is about to explode. She's a total bride monster. "Oh. My. Glob. Are you *really* trying to *ruin my wedding day!?*"

LSP's father is not pleased with what's going down. After all, Lumpy Space Weddings are crazy expensive, and now this tiny robot is junking the whole thing up! "BMO, this is a *serious* accusation," he says." Do you have evidence?"

"Of course I have confirmation of my strange tale!" BMO says. "The Earl of Lemongrab is a big—"

And with that, BMO presses play, all ready to put the kibosh on the earl's dastardly plans.

But the sound is garbled!

The recording was damaged in the fall!

Now, the entire chapel is staring at BMO, watching and waiting . . .

★ ★ **BMO earns 27 ADVENTURE MINUTES.** ★ ★

HELP BMO EXPOSE THE EARL OF LEMONGRAB!

Draw straight lines connecting each of the BMOs in the drawing below. Cross out any letters your lines pass through. The remaining letters will tell you what BMO should say.

If BMO should tell everyone that Lemongrab is a PHONY, **TURN TO PAGE 52**

If BMO should tell everyone that Lemongrab is a CROOK, **TURN TO PAGE 75**

DEATH IS A KUNG-FU KICK FIST MASTER!

Finally, BMO can take no more. And since BMO *IS the video-game system,* BMO can make anything happen! Y'know, like let Death win . . . And BMO does just that.

Moments later, Death is conquering *Kung-Fu Kick Fist's* final boss. "Yes!" Death exclaims. "I am *awesome* at this game."

BMO grins.

"Now that that's done," Death says as he sets down the controller, "it's time we addressed the issue of that soul, eh?"

BMO smiles. "Yes, please!"

Death grins and waves his hand in the air and *POOF!*—from out of nowhere, a strange, magical window appears. Through the window BMO sees *souls!* They are small glowing forms: blue and red and green and yellow and purple. And there are *tons* of the little souls.

"Do you like what you see?" Death asks with a grin.

BMO nods. "I do!"

Death waves his hands and the window changes. It's now showing *live* action. "And look here—it looks like THIS young boy's soul will soon be mine."

With horror, BMO sees that the window is showing *Finn!* Death has opened a portal-window-thing into the Land of Ooo!

BMO sees Finn lying on his back. Above him is a giant,

wormlike creature. BMO doesn't yet know it, but the creature is actually the strange monstrosity known as the Wormenstein. And Finn is about to be crushed beneath it . . .

"This little blond creature is in *big* trouble," Death says. "It appears he will be dead in moments. And then his soul will belong to me . . ."

"Oh no," BMO whispers. "Finn . . ."

"Well, what it'll be, little one?" Death asks.

WHAT SHOULD BMO DO?

Circle each letter that has an beneath it.
Then read the circled letters to spell out what
BMO wants to do!

DKSDAEGVMEZXTOP

YRYFDQIRNDNEQGD

If you agree with BMO's decision,
TURN TO PAGE 105

If you don't agree with BMO decision,
TURN TO PAGE 11

THROUGH THE
PORTAL TO SAVE FINN

"I must save my friend!" BMO exclaims.

BMO's little legs move as fast as they can, and BMO *leaps* through the portal and back into the Land of the Living—*the real world*—The Land of Ooo. The portal has spit BMO out high above *anything* and BMO is somersaulting through the sky, down toward the Candy Kingdom.

BMO spots the Wormenstein, the giant worm monster that was about to kill Finn just a second before—*SHMACK!*—BMO lands atop the thing! This strange creature is made *entirely* of other, regular worms! There are thousands upon thousands of tiny little green worms writhing around, somehow joined together by Princess Bubblegum's mad science.

BMO hangs on as the Wormenstein thrashes around, just moments from crushing Finn. BMO needs to do something! So the tiny robot reaches out and *pinches* the worm's yucky wet flesh. The Wormenstein *howls!* It can feel pain! BMO then reaches in and grabs a handful of worms and *rips* them out.

Just then, Jake throws his rubbery arms out and grabs Finn. "C'mon, bro!" Jake shouts, and with a *tug*, pulls Finn away from the danger.

The Wormenstein falls forward and crashes to the ground where Finn was lying just seconds ago. A moment earlier and the Wormenstein would have **crushed** Finn. BMO saved him!

As the Wormenstein hits the ground, BMO is tossed aside and skitters to a stop at Finn's feet.

"BMO!" Finn exclaims. "That was you? You saved my life!"

BMO is dizzy and seeing sparks, but manages to squeak out, "Yes. BMO saved you. BMO is a hero!"

But the adventure is not over . . .

The Wormenstein turns . . .

It's angry . . .

How can BMO, Finn, and Jake battle this huge creature?

BMO has an idea . . .

★ ★ **BMO earns 41 ADVENTURE MINUTES.** ★ ★

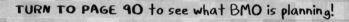

TURN TO PAGE 90 to see what BMO is planning!

BMO'S
BACK!

Marceline holds her breath (which is really just an old habit, because she's a vampire and vampires obviously don't need to breathe).

After a long moment, BMO's screen flashes, then two eyes appear! BMO is back online!

"Hello!" BMO says. "I am returned!"

Melissa shrieks. "*Oh. My. Glob.* That was *amazing!*"

"Y'know what, I think I'll drive the rest of the way," Marceline says.

"I think that is a smart strategy," BMO says.

★ ★ **BMO earns 21 ADVENTURE MINUTES.** ★ ★

BMO's back, baby! But the adventure isn't over...
TURN TO PAGE 99

WRONG, YOU FOOL!

It's not Tree Trunks, it's Peppermint Butler!

"BMO, you don't recognize me?" Peppermint Butler asks.

BMO frowns. "Sorry, Pep-But."

"I was going to help you retrieve a soul from the Land of the Dead and become a real boy."

"Really?" BMO asks. "Let's go!"

"No. Not now."

"Please?" BMO begs.

Peppermint Butler's eyes narrow and his face gets all *dark* and *scary* and little fangs appear. "I said **NO!**"

With that, Peppermint Butler turns and hops out the window, leaving BMO alone. Sadly, now BMO will never be a real boy . . .

THE END

VISITORS!

BMO lets Death continue playing. If Death is going to beat *Kung-Fu Kick Fist*, BMO believes it should go down honestly, no cheating.

Much time passes.

Days.

Weeks.

Months.

Years?

BMO is not sure. It is all a blur of Kung-Fu kick fisting.

But then, one lonely day, a voice! *A familiar voice.*

"Holy Schmow! It's BMO!"

BMO spins. It's Finn and Jake, coming over the hill! BMO has never been so happy . . .

Is BMO saved at last? To find out,
TURN TO PAGE 24

PEPPERMINT BUTLER,
THE CREEPY CREEP

It's Peppermint Butler!

"*Hello!*" Peppermint Butler says. Peppermint Butler has a voice like a classy old British dude. "BMO, if you want a soul, you just ask Death! Death and I are old friends."

BMO's screen lights up. "Okay, Pep-But!"

Now Death, of course, lives in the Land of the Dead. And you can't just stroll in through the front door, 'cause it's the Land of the Dead, and that means it's full of dead folks and you'll end up dead, too. That's just how it goes. But Peppermint Butler knows a secret . . .

"Just concentrate on the point where the two walls meet, then cross your eyes," Peppermint Butler tells BMO.

BMO's eyes cross *very* tight. Suddenly, the point where the walls meet *opens*, revealing a magical, mysterious door! Through the door, BMO sees a strange, scary world full of floating platforms made of rock and a dark, blood red sky. It is *THE LAND OF THE DEAD*.

And it is totes scary . . .

★ ★ **BMO earns 9 ADVENTURE MINUTES.** ★ ★

110

If you think BMO should step through the magical door and into the Land of the Dead, **TURN TO PAGE 79**

If you think this is nuts and BMO is better off trying to catch up to Finn and Jake, **TURN TO PAGE 21**

DOWN IN THE DUNGEON!

"Worms, bring these sleepy citizens to the dungeon," the King Worm says.

A thousand worms begin pushing and guiding BMO, Finn, Jake, and the citizens of the Candy Kingdom inside the castle walls.

The gang is led through the streets of the Candy Kingdom. BMO waddles along, trying very hard to look asleep. They pass tiny candy homes before being led into the castle and down into the dark, dank dungeon (made of chocolate, of course). Lastly, the worms usher them all inside a prison cell, and the door clangs shut.

Finn and Jake stand perfectly still, staring out of the bars. They're snoozing. Everyone is in a dream trance! Everyone except BMO . . .

But how to escape!? How to free the princess?

And then BMO has a very smart idea.

Flattery!

BMO waddles to the bars, where two Banana Guards are standing watch. "You Banana Guards are very handsome," BMO says. "I am a camera, too! Say cheese and I will take your snapshot."

One Banana Guard smiles. "Um, yes, please! I love photos."

"Great!" BMO says.

BMO's camera flashes—and the guards are blinded by the bright light! When the flash fades and they can finally see again, they realize something is wrong . . .

HELP BMO ESCAPE!

Here's what the two Banana Guards looked like before BMO took the photo, and here's what they look like now. How many things are missing or changed?

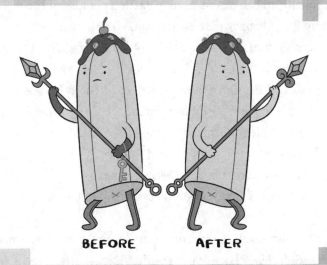

BEFORE   **AFTER**

If you think there are four things missing,
TURN TO PAGE 64

If you think there are five things missing,
TURN TO PAGE 20

MEETING
DEATH

BMO and Peppermint Butler walk until their feet are sore—traveling across the deathly plains and over dark mountains and past armies of hungry skeletons.

Finally, in the distance, they catch a glimpse of their goal. "There it is," Peppermint Butler says. "Death's castle."

Death's castle is made entirely of *light*. In fact, it's the only bright thing in the Land of Death. Death is cool like that.

BMO and Pep-But follow the River of Forgetfulness up to the castle and through its front gate, then past a Zen garden filled with skulls to a small hut made all of bone. Inside the hut, Death is curled up on a simple bed, snoring.

"Aw, he's doing sleeps," BMO whispers.

"He's on his Death Bed," Peppermint Butler says with a shrug.

BMO waddles closer and tugs on the comforter—made entirely of *skin*—that covers Death. "Excuse me, Death? Mr. Death?"

Death snorts and coughs and then, when BMO tugs harder, Death wakes. His big eyes dart around the hut and at last land on BMO. "Who? What? What do you want?! Who dares enter the castle of Death without knocking at Death's Door?"

BMO is trembling. "Um, well, Death, sir, you see . . ."

But BMO is saved! Death spots Peppermint Butler. "Oh, Peppermint Butler!" Death exclaims. "*What* is the good word?!"

"We have come to the Land of the Dead in hopes of acquiring the soul of a young boy for my friend BMO," Pep-But explains.

Death nods his big, fat skull head. "Ah, one of those '*I want to be a real boy!*' Pinocchio deals?"

Death climbs out of bed and throws on a robe. It's pink and pale and—*eww*—just like the comforter, *it's made of skin.*

BMO takes a step back. Maybe this was a bad idea. But it's too late to turn back now . . .

Death kneels down and stares into the screen of the tiny robot. "A soul is very serious business. Are you totally 100 percent positive you want one? No take backs in the Land of the Dead."

BMO nods once. "Yes."

"Then we shall play a game," Death says.

Oh no . . . BMO wonders what sort of game Death will want to play. Something macabre and terrible, surely—something dark and dreadful.

"Do you have *Kung-Fu Kick Fist?*" Death asks excitedly. "I *love Kung-Fu Kick Fist!*"

Wait. What?! Death wants to play video games? BMO is ecstatic. That's not scary! "Yes, I do have *Kung-Fu Kick Fist,*" BMO says proudly.

"Woo-hoo! Let's play!"

BMO takes a seat

and flips on *Kung-Fu Kick Fist*, then pulls out a joystick and hands it to Death. Death sits cross-legged in front of the tiny robot.

Only problem?

BMO soon realizes that Death is *terrible* at *Kung-Fu Kick Fist*.

"Aw, c'mon!" Death shouts. "The controller messed me up! What is there, peanut butter on here or something?"

BMO frowns as Death dives back into the world of *Kung-Fu Kick Fist*. Again, Death gets his butt handed to him.

"This is bunk!" Death shouts. "Something is definitely up with this controller. The timing is all off."

BMO is starting to get nervous.

Death narrows his eyes. "All right, once more—and I'm warning you, BMO, I'm going to be *very* upset if I don't win . . ."

★ ✴ **BMO earns 18 ADVENTURE MINUTES.** ★ ✴

HELP DEATH BEAT *KUNG-FU KICK FIST*

Guide Death through the maze to reach the giant spider and deliver a killer blow!

If Death reaches the spider,
TURN TO PAGE 93

If Death loses,
TURN TO PAGE 97

NO SOUL, BUT
LOTS OF FRIENDS

Jake comes through the portal and crashes to the ground. The safe ground! The ground back in the normal world, the Land of Ooo! But before he can celebrate, Finn is tumbling on top of him, face to butt.

BMO comes through last. The tiny robot hits the ground and rolls over. There's mud on BMO's screen. With a smile, Finn gently wipes it off.

"Cool stuff, dudes," Jake says as he rolls over onto his butt. "We made it!"

Finn and Jake both have wide grins on their faces. But BMO does not . . .

"Hey, what's the matter, BMO?" Finn asks.

BMO doesn't say anything. BMO just sits, staring at the ground.

"BMO bud, spill it," Jake urges.

"I wanted to be a real boy," BMO says.

Jake nods his head. "Oh right, you didn't get your soul. Maybe that's best—you always end up doing weird junk when you're left alone."

Finn glares at Jake. Jake just shrugs.

Finn leans down and picks up his tiny robot friend. "No, BMO, you're not a real boy. But you *are* a **real friend**. And I think that's good enough."

    Jake frowns. "You two are supercorny."

★ ✹ **BMO** *earns* 50 ADVENTURE MINUTES. ★ ✹

THE END

WHAT's YOUR ADVENTURE TIME?

Slamacow!

It's time to add up all those Adventure Minutes you earned and figure out your grand-lumping-total **Adventure Time**.

So, how did you do? Did you stop LSP's wedding? Did you save the Candy Kingdom from the clutches of the King Worm? Did you get BMO the soul that the tiny robot craved so badly?

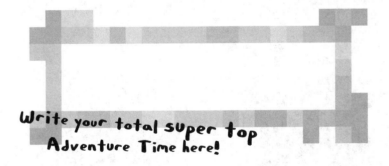

Write your total super top Adventure Time here!

Want to increase your Adventure Time? Flip back to page one and begin the adventure again, making new choices until you get the *maximum* Adventure Time!

ANSWERS

PG 14

PG 31

PG 34

WORM

PG 59

PG 66

PG 69

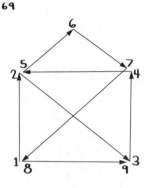

PG 81

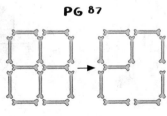

CANYON

PG 77

PG 87

remove 2 bones

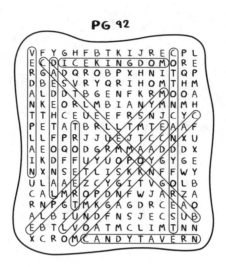

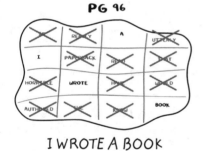

I WROTE A BOOK

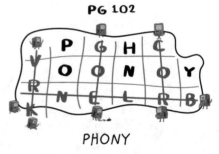

PHONY

SAVE FINN

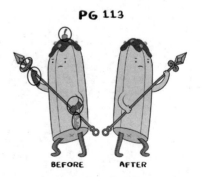

BEFORE   AFTER